Too Much Noise

Too Much Noise

by Ann McGovern

illustrated by Simms Taback

Houghton Mifflin Company Boston

Also by
ANN McGOVERN
Who Has a Secret?

LIBRARY OF CONGRESS CATALOG CARD NUMBER: AC 67-10562

RNF ISBN 0-395-18110-0   PA ISBN 0-395-62985-3

PRINTED IN CHINA

SCP   50 49 48 47 46 45 44

4500573011

To DD with love

A long time ago there was an old man.
His name was Peter, and he lived in an old, old house.

The bed creaked.

The floor squeaked.

Outside, the wind blew the leaves through the tre

The leaves fell on the roof. *Swish. Swish.*

The tea kettle whistled. *Hiss. Hiss.*

"Too noisy," said Peter.

Peter went to see the wise man of the village.
"What can I do?" Peter asked the wise man.
"My house makes too much noise.
My bed creaks.
My floor squeaks.
The wind blows the leaves through the trees.
The leaves fall on the roof. *Swish. Swish.*
My tea kettle whistles. *Hiss. Hiss.*"

"I can help you," the wise man said. "I know what you can do."
"What?" said Peter.
"Get a cow," said the wise man.

"What good is a cow?" said Peter.
 But Peter got a cow anyhow.

went home ...
 ∧
 and

The cow said, "Moo. MOO."
The bed creaked.
The floor squeaked.
The leaves fell on the roof. *Swish. Swish.*
The tea kettle whistled. *Hiss. Hiss.*

all

"Too noisy," said Peter.
 And he went back to the wise man.
"Get a donkey," said the wise man.
"What good is a donkey?" said Peter.
 But Peter got a donkey anyhow.

went home ...
and

The donkey said, "HEE-Haw."
The cow said, "Moo. MOO."
The bed creaked.
The floor squeaked.
The leaves fell on the roof. *Swish. Swish.*
The tea kettle whistled. *Hiss. Hiss.*

"Still too noisy," said Peter.
  And he went back to the wise man.

"Get a sheep," said the wise man.
"What good is a sheep?" said Peter.
  But Peter got a sheep anyhow.

went home...
and

The sheep said, "Baa. Baa."
The donkey said, "HEE-Haw."
The cow said, "Moo. MOO."
The bed creaked.
The floor squeaked.
The leaves fell on the roof. *Swish*. *Swish*.
The tea kettle whistled. *Hiss*. *Hiss*.

all

went home...
and

"Too noisy," said Peter.
And he went back to the wise man.

"Get a hen," said the wise man.
"What good is a hen?" said Peter.
But Peter got a hen anyhow.

The hen said, "Cluck. Cluck."
The sheep said, "Baa. Baa."
The donkey said, "HEE-Haw."
The cow said, "Moo. MOO."
The bed creaked.
The floor squeaked.
The leaves fell on the roof. *Swish. Swish.*
The tea kettle whistled. *Hiss. Hiss.*

"Too noisy," said Peter.
And back he went to the wise man.

"Get a dog," the wise man said.
"And get a cat too."
"What good is a dog?" said Peter.
"Or a cat?"
But Peter got a dog and a cat anyhow.

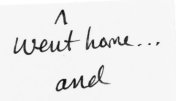
went home...
and

The dog said, "Woof. Woof."
The cat said, "Mee-ow. Mee-ow."
The hen said, "Cluck. Cluck."
The sheep said, "Baa. Baa."
The donkey said, "HEE-Haw."
The cow said, "Moo. MOO."
The bed creaked.
The floor squeaked.
The leaves fell on the roof. *Swish. Swish.*
The tea kettle whistled. *Hiss. Hiss.*

Now Peter was angry.

He went to the wise man.

"I told you my house was too noisy," he said.

"I told you my bed creaks.

My floor squeaks.

The leaves fall on the roof. *Swish. Swish.*

The tea kettle whistles. *Hiss. Hiss.*

You told me to get a cow.

All day the cow says, 'Moo. MOO.'

You told me to get a donkey.

All day the donkey says, 'HEE-Haw.'

You told me to get a sheep.

All day the sheep says, 'Baa. Baa.'

You told me to get a hen.

All day the hen says, 'Cluck. Cluck.'

You told me to get a dog.

And a cat.

All day the dog says, 'Woof. Woof.'

All day the cat says, 'Mee-ow. Mee-ow.'

I am going crazy," said Peter.

35

The wise man said, "Do what I tell you.
Let the cow go.
Let the donkey go.
Let the sheep go.
Let the hen go.
Let the dog go.
Let the cat go."

So Peter let the cow go.
He let the donkey go.
He let the sheep go.
He let the hen go.
He let the dog go.
He let the cat go.

all —
drop out
when called

Now no cow said, "Moo. MOO."
No donkey said, "HEE-Haw."
No sheep said, "Baa. Baa."
No hen said, "Cluck. Cluck."
No dog said, "Woof. Woof."
No cat said, "Mee-ow. Mee-ow."

The bed creaked.

"Ah," said Peter. "What a quiet noise."

The floor squeaked.

"Oh," said Peter. "What a quiet noise."

Outside the leaves fell on the roof. *Swish. Swish.*

Inside the tea kettle whistled. *Hiss. Hiss.*

"Ah. Oh," said Peter. "How quiet my house is."

And Peter got into his bed and went to sleep
and dreamed a very
                    quiet
                         dream.